The Creature From Outer Space

"Andy is awfully brave. I'll never make fun of him again," Jessica said.

"*If* he makes it back alive," Charlie said.

"Look!" Lila gasped.

They all turned to look again. The alien was pointing in the direction from which it had come.

"He must be pointing toward his spaceship," Todd whispered.

"Andy isn't going with him, is he?" Elizabeth asked fearfully.

As they all watched, the alien put its arm across Andy's shoulders.

"He's being kidnapped!" Lila moaned.

Bantam Skylark Books in the SWEET VALLEY KIDS series

SWEET VALLEY KIDS

ANDY AND THE ALIEN

Written by
Molly Mia Stewart

Created by
FRANCINE PASCAL

Illustrated by
Ying-Hwa Hu

A BANTAM SKYLARK BOOK®
NEW YORK · TORONTO · LONDON · SYDNEY · AUCKLAND

RL 2, 005–008

ANDY AND THE ALIEN
A Bantam Skylark Book / May 1992

*Sweet Valley High® and Sweet Valley Kids are
trademarks of Francine Pascal*

Conceived by Francine Pascal

*Produced by Daniel Weiss Associates, Inc.
33 West 17th Street
New York, NY 10011*

Cover art by Susan Tang

*Skylark Books is a registered trademark of Bantam Books, a
division of Bantam Doubleday Dell Publishing Group, Inc.
Registered in U.S. Patent and Trademark Office and elsewhere.*

ISBN 0-553-15925-9

Published simultaneously in the United States and Canada

*Bantam Books are published by Bantam Books, a division of Ban-
tam Doubleday Dell Publishing Group, Inc. Its trademark,
consisting of the words "Bantam Books" and the portrayal of a
rooster, is Registered in U.S. Patent and Trademark Office and in
other countries. Marca Registrada. Bantam Books, 666 Fifth Ave-
nue, New York, New York 10103.*

PRINTED IN THE UNITED STATES OF AMERICA

OPM   0 9 8 7 6 5 4 3 2 1

To Jacob Copskey

CHAPTER 1

Unidentified Flying Objects

"I hope we win lots of ribbons on Field Day tomorrow," Jessica Wakefield said. She and her twin sister, Elizabeth, were practicing for the three-legged race while they waited for the school bus. Jessica had tied her left leg to her sister's right leg with a hair ribbon.

"Me, too," Elizabeth replied. "We're sure to win first prize in the three-legged race if we concentrate."

"Remember to count while we're running," Jessica said. "That will help us stay together."

Elizabeth and Jessica were the best pair of three-legged racers in second grade. They always said that it was because they were identical twins. They were used to sharing everything, so it was easy for them to work together as a team. Being identical twins meant that they even shared their looks. Both girls had blue-green eyes and long blonde hair with bangs. Sometimes the only way their friends could tell them apart was by looking at the name bracelets the twins always wore.

Many people expected Elizabeth and Jessica to be identical on the inside like they were on the outside. But that wasn't so. They had very different personalities and interests. Elizabeth liked reading and playing sports, and she was a member of the Sweet Valley Soccer League. No one ever had to remind her to do her homework, because she loved school. Jessica liked school, too, but only because it was such a good place to see all her friends. She preferred playing with her dollhouse to playing soccer. These differences didn't matter to the twins, though. They knew that they would always be best friends.

"Here comes the bus," Elizabeth said.

"Let's see if we can get on with our legs still tied together," Jessica suggested.

"OK," Elizabeth said, giggling. "I just hope we can both fit through the door at the same time!"

The bus pulled up to the curb, and the driver opened the door.

3

"Come on, Liz, here we go," Jessica said. "One-two, one-two!"

The twins tried to climb up the bus steps. But when Jessica lifted her right foot, Elizabeth tried to step up with *her* right foot, which was tied to Jessica's left foot. So Jessica found herself halfway up the first step, while her sister was still on the sidewalk.

Then Jessica tried to lift her left foot and Elizabeth's right foot up, while Elizabeth was trying to step up with her left foot. Finally, Elizabeth tried hopping up with both feet at once and ended up wedged on the step next to Jessica.

The bus driver, Ms. Manfredi, smiled as she watched them. "I can tell it's almost Field Day," she said. "I just hope that a bus isn't part of the course for the three-legged race, or you girls are in big trouble."

The girls laughed. "Me, too," they both said at the same time. They untied their legs and climbed aboard.

All of the kids on the bus were talking about Field Day. Field Day was a special event which was held every year. The whole school went to nearby Secca Lake for a day of picnicking, games, contests, and nature walks. Elizabeth and Jessica had been looking forward to it for weeks.

When the twins got to school, Elizabeth went to put her books on her desk. As she did, she heard loud laughter coming from the front of the room. She went to see what was going on. Andy Franklin was sitting at his desk, surrounded by several kids, including Jessica.

Lila Fowler was there, too. "Look out, Andy," she said loudly. She tossed a paper airplane at him. "A Martian UFO might land on you." Lila was Jessica's best friend after Elizabeth.

"Then you'll turn green, and it'll vaporize you," Charlie Cashman said. "Zap!"

Jessica laughed and started making her own paper airplane. "Be careful, Andy. This one's from Venus!"

Andy was serious and very smart. He wore glasses, and they were always falling off during gym class.

Elizabeth thought that Andy was nice. She liked talking to him about science. It was one of her favorite subjects, and Andy knew more about it than anyone else in the whole second grade. Jessica didn't like Andy very much, though, because she thought he was too nerdy.

Usually Andy was quiet and nobody

teased him, but for the past few days, he had been bringing in books about UFOs. A lot of the kids in class thought that was silly, and they started making fun of him whenever he talked about aliens or outer space.

"Do you think we'll see any UFOs at Secca Lake tomorrow?" Jessica asked Andy. She tried to look very serious.

"Maybe. Look at these newspaper clippings," Andy said. He pulled some papers out of one of his books. "A lot of people have reported seeing lights and hearing strange noises up there."

Jessica couldn't keep a straight face. She burst out laughing. "I hear a strange noise right now. It's coming from right there," she said, pointing at Andy.

The other kids laughed.

7

"Why do they tease him so much?" Elizabeth asked Amy Sutton, who had just walked into the room.

Amy made a face. "He's too serious about everything," she said. "Anyway, believing in UFOs is kind of dumb. Everybody knows there's no such thing. Hey, look at Ken."

Ken Matthews was holding his hands up to his head and wiggling his fingers like antennae. "Warning! Warning!" he said in a robot voice. "Earth is being invaded by monster aliens."

"I think there's a good chance that alien visitors would be friendly," Andy insisted. "They would probably want to make friends with us and learn about our planet."

"Well, I wouldn't invite any aliens to my birthday party, that's for sure," Lila said.

"Why not?" Andy asked. "I think it would be interesting."

"The aliens would love to go to Andy's party," Charlie said. "They'd have a lot in common with him. They're all out of this world!" The others laughed again.

"If we meet any aliens at Secca Lake tomorrow, *you* can make contact with them," Jessica told Andy, giggling. "And *you* can bring them in for Show and Tell."

Andy looked excited. "I hope we do meet some extraterrestrial visitors at Secca Lake! My equipment is all ready."

Jessica looked over at Elizabeth and rolled her eyes.

Elizabeth shook her head. She had a feeling that Field Day was going to be very interesting.

CHAPTER 2

All Aboard

After Mrs. Otis took attendance the next morning, everyone went outside to wait for the buses that were going to take them to Secca Lake. All of the kids in Sweet Valley Elementary were lined up with their grades, and everyone was talking and laughing with excitement.

Jessica unzipped her knapsack for the third time. Her lunch and Elizabeth's were inside, along with their sweaters and some extra juice boxes. "Who should carry this first?" she asked.

"I will," Elizabeth offered.

"Good." Jessica smiled. She could carry it later, when it was empty and light.

"OK, class, here's our bus. Please quiet down," Mrs. Otis called out. Their teacher was wearing jeans and sneakers and a red T-shirt. She checked her attendance list again as everyone climbed aboard the bus.

Jessica and Elizabeth sat together in one of the front seats. Ellen Riteman and Lila sat down behind them.

"Look at Andy," Ellen said, poking Jessica in the shoulder.

Andy was having a difficult time getting up the steps of the bus. He had a camera slung over one shoulder, and a portable cas-

sette recorder on a strap over his other shoulder. He was holding his lunch bag in one hand and his UFO books in the other.

"Do you need a hand, Andy?" Mrs. Otis asked him.

"No, thanks," he said. One of his books slipped onto the floor, and when he bent over to pick it up, his glasses fell off.

Jessica began to laugh. "Is all that stuff your UFO equipment?"

"Of course," Andy said. He finally made it to the top of the steps and started trying to make his way down the aisle.

"Ouch!" Lila shouted as his camera bumped her on the arm. "Watch out!"

Jessica still couldn't believe that Andy was serious about looking for UFOs. "Are you going to take pictures of aliens?" she asked him.

"If I see any," Andy said, smiling eagerly. "And record them, too. I hope they can speak English."

"Oh, brother," Ellen said.

"He's a wacko," Jessica whispered to her sister.

Elizabeth shrugged. "How do you know we won't see anything?" she asked. "Andy knows a lot more about science than any of us."

As Andy looked for a seat on the bus, his UFO equipment kept knocking into people. Finally, he found a seat. It took him a few minutes to put all of his things down. While he was adjusting his camera strap, Charlie quietly leaned across the aisle and took Andy's lunch bag. Jessica giggled and nudged Lila.

"What?" Lila whispered.

"Charlie took Andy's lunch," Jessica whispered back.

Elizabeth turned around quickly. "That's mean," she said.

"Shh!" Jessica and Lila both said at the same time.

"Hey," Andy spoke up suddenly. He was looking around with a puzzled expression. "Where's my lunch?"

Charlie shrugged. "Maybe an alien took it."

"There goes the UFO!" Jerry McAllister shouted, pointing out the window. "Stop them! They have Andy's lunch."

Andy frowned. "Come on, you guys. Give me back my lunch."

"Come on, you guys. Give me back my lunch," Charlie said, imitating Andy's voice.

By this time everyone on the bus was

16

watching. Caroline Pearce got up and headed toward Mrs. Otis, who was talking to the bus driver.

"She's going to tell," Ellen said grumpily. "Caroline is such a tattletale."

Caroline pointed to the back of the bus and explained to the teacher what had happened. Mrs. Otis stood up. "We're not leaving this parking lot until Andy gets his lunch back," she announced.

Jessica was suddenly on Andy's side. "Give him his lunch back," she said, bouncing up and down with impatience. "We don't want to be late." The sooner they got to Secca Lake, she thought, the sooner the Field Day games could begin.

CHAPTER 3

Field Day

Elizabeth spun around in a circle and then did a handstand. "Isn't it nice up here?" she asked as she flopped back onto the grass next to her sister.

Secca Lake sparkled in the sunshine, and grassy fields spread in all directions. Birds sang in the nearby woods.

"Look," Jessica said, pointing. "The fifth graders are leaving on their nature walk. And I heard that the third graders get to go on a survival trail, with ropes to climb, and tunnels, and skinny bridges you have to walk across."

Elizabeth nodded. "We'll get to do that next year. I can't wait."

Mr. Cutler, the gym teacher, blew his whistle. "Second graders! Line up for the sack race!"

"Come on!" Elizabeth jumped to her feet and grabbed Jessica's hand.

"Watch me win this one," Ken Matthews bragged as they all formed a line. "I'm an expert."

"Expert show-off," Winston Egbert said.

Everyone was excited about starting the games. Elizabeth smiled at Jessica as Mr. Cutler began handing out large burlap bags. Elizabeth stepped into hers and held it up to her waist. Some of the kids were practicing

19

by hopping back and forth. Mrs. Otis walked to the other end of the field with a red flag.

"One line, please," Mr. Cutler called out.

Elizabeth glanced to her left. Andy was having trouble keeping his burlap bag from getting tangled under his feet. Luckily, he had put his camera and tape recorder down on the ground. Mrs. Otis wouldn't let him play games with them around his shoulders. While Elizabeth watched, Charlie and Jerry hopped closer to Andy.

"I hope they don't try to trip him," she said to Jessica.

"Don't worry about Andy," Jessica said. "Just try to win, OK? If we get some ribbons, we can hang them up in our room."

"On your marks, get set, GO!" Mr. Cutler yelled.

All the second graders began hopping across the grass toward Mrs. Otis. Elizabeth held her bag up tight so it wouldn't trip her. Ellen screamed as Amy bumped into her, but neither of them fell down. Then Andy stumbled and lost his grip on his bag. He tumbled headfirst to the ground.

"Look out!" Charlie yelled. "It's the klutz from Mars!"

Elizabeth was hopping as fast as she could toward the finish line. She felt sorry for Andy, but she knew there was still time for him to catch up. Ahead of her, she saw Todd Wilkins and Amy Sutton out in front of everybody else, hopping side by side. Elizabeth was in third place. She lunged after Todd and Amy, trying to catch up to them.

"Come on!" Mrs. Otis yelled, waving them all on.

Gritting her teeth, Elizabeth put on a burst of speed. Then Amy's bag slipped, and she had to stop to fix it. Elizabeth passed her, but Todd was still ahead.

"It's a close race," Mrs. Otis yelled, raising the red flag above her head. "But the winner is . . ."

Just as Elizabeth hopped her longest hop, Todd crossed the finish line, and Mrs. Otis dropped the red flag. Elizabeth crossed second, followed by Amy. One by one, the others hopped across, too. Jessica came in fifth, right behind Ken.

"Did you see Andy?" Ken asked her as they dropped their bags around their ankles and stepped out of them.

"I told you," Charlie said, hopping up beside them. "He's a klutz from Mars."

Andy, who was nearby, heard what Charlie said and shook his head. He had been one of the last to finish the race. "Scientists haven't found proof of life on any of the other planets in our solar system so far."

The boys all laughed.

Elizabeth felt sorry for Andy. She wanted to say something to defend him, since the others were being so mean. "You fell down, too, Winston," she pointed out.

"Yeah, but I'm still an earthling," Winston said. "Besides, I think the reason I fell was Andy tripped me with his Martian laser beam."

The other boys laughed again.

Elizabeth just shook her head and walked away.

After handing out ribbons for first, second, and third place, Mrs. Otis announced that it was time for the egg toss. Charlie punched Andy in the arm. "Hey, want to be my partner?" he asked.

"Sure," Andy said happily.

"What now?" Elizabeth muttered, expecting the worst.

The students formed two lines, with partners facing each other. Mrs. Otis handed a raw egg to each team, and the kids began tossing the eggs back and forth. After each toss, each partner took a step back. When the lines were five feet apart, some people began missing their catches. Lila tossed her egg to Ellen, who dropped it. The egg landed on the grass and cracked open.

"Back up farther," Charlie said to Andy.

"OK." Andy was concentrating hard on catching the egg.

Then, Charlie took aim and threw the egg right at Andy's chest. It splattered on Andy's shirt, and raw egg dripped down all over his clothes.

"I don't know what happened," Charlie said, laughing. "An alien must have taken over my aim!"

Andy took a tissue out of his shorts pocket and wiped off as much of the dripping yolk and egg white as he could. "You'll see, Charlie," he said in quiet voice. "You can make fun of me as much as you want to now. But one day you may believe in aliens, too."

CHAPTER 4

Into the Woods

By lunchtime, Jessica's stomach was growling with hunger. "I'm starved!" she said as she sat down on the grass next to her sister.

"Me, too," Elizabeth agreed. She opened the knapsack and handed Jessica a sandwich and a juice box.

"Sit with us," Jessica said as Lila and Ellen walked up.

Eva Simpson and Amy sat down with them,

too. Nearby, a group of boys were clowning around as they ate their lunches. Andy was standing alone, looking for a place to sit.

"Isn't he the goofiest?" Lila asked.

"He really thinks there are UFOs up here," Ellen said, shaking her head. "That is so stupid."

"Hey, Andy," Jessica called. "What did you bring for lunch? Space rocks?"

Ellen and Lila both giggled. Elizabeth didn't think it was very funny.

"No, just a peanut butter and jelly sandwich," Andy answered.

Charlie and some of the other boys began teasing him again. They pretended to be aliens shooting each other with ray guns. Andy ignored them. He sat by himself, reading his UFO book and eating his lunch. Finally, he picked up his camera and tape recorder and walked away.

"Where are you going?" Jessica asked. "Searching for UFOs?"

Andy looked back at her and nodded. "Yes."

"Ooohh! Can I come?" Jessica asked.

Andy didn't answer. He kept heading toward the woods. Jessica watched him, her eyes sparkling with mischief. "Come on," she said to Lila.

They stood up and followed him. Charlie stuck out one foot to trip them as they passed. "Quit it," Jessica said. "We're following Andy to see if he finds any alien spaceships."

"I'll go with you," Charlie said, jumping to his feet. "This is going to be fun."

Jessica looked back over her shoulder. She saw that Elizabeth and Todd had gotten up to follow them, too. "Watch this," Jessica whispered to Charlie and Lila.

She picked a long blade of grass and ran up behind Andy. She tickled him on the back of the neck with the grass stem. When Andy spun around, she gave him an innocent look.

"It was an alien," she explained.

Charlie and Lila both laughed. Andy just shoved his glasses up his nose and kept on walking.

"What are you doing?" Elizabeth asked as she and Todd caught up.

"We want to see the aliens," Jessica explained. "Who knows, maybe they'll look just like Andy."

Twigs crackled underfoot as they all walked into the woods single file. Andy was

ahead of the others. He walked quickly, but looked around carefully as he went.

"How far are you going?" Jessica called out to him.

"Until I find some signs of UFOs," Andy said.

After a few more minutes, Jessica began to feel tired and thirsty. She wanted to drink her second juice box, but she had left it behind. Charlie was hitting trees with a stick as he walked, and Jessica was afraid that he would hit her with it by accident.

"Let's go back," she said to Lila and Elizabeth.

"OK," Lila agreed. "I'm bored."

"No," Elizabeth said firmly. "We have to stay with Andy."

Jessica looked surprised. "Why? You don't

think he's really going to find any UFOs, do you?"

"No," Elizabeth said. "But I think we should all stick together."

"That's right," Todd said. "If we split up, some of us might get lost."

Jessica hadn't thought of that. As she looked around at the dense forest surrounding them on all sides, she realized that she wasn't sure exactly how to get back to the lake. Also, she began to hear strange sounds coming from the trees. The sounds were probably just birds, she thought—but then again, she couldn't be certain. She began to feel worried. What if they were lost already?

Suddenly, she had an even scarier thought. What if there really *were* aliens in the woods, after all?

CHAPTER 5

Invaders From Space

"I still think we should go back," Jessica told Elizabeth.

"You can go," Elizabeth said. "I'm staying with Andy." Elizabeth was angry with Jessica for teasing Andy so much. She was also afraid that they were already lost. She turned around and saw a bright light up ahead through the trees. "Is that a clearing?" she asked.

"I think so," Andy said. He adjusted his

camera and his tape recorder. "There could be something there."

The others followed Andy and Elizabeth to the edge of the clearing. Just beyond the trees they saw a large, sunny meadow.

"Look at all those daisies," Elizabeth said. "They're pretty."

Meanwhile Jessica was looking toward the center of the meadow. "What's that?" she whispered. Her finger was shaking as she pointed at a group of strange-looking objects. They were too far away to see clearly.

"I'm going to explore," Andy announced, stepping out into the meadow.

"I'll go with you," Elizabeth said. Todd followed them.

"Wait up," Jessica said. She headed after them, with Lila and Charlie right behind her. All six of them walked across the meadow through the daisies and tall grass, until they were close enough to see the strange objects better.

"Wow," Elizabeth whispered, wide-eyed. She walked a bit closer to the objects. "It looks like some kind of scientific equipment."

The others nodded. Jessica saw that there was a dish antenna that turned from side to side, and various things with needles and gadgets that spun or swayed back and forth. There was a tall skinny object that looked like a lamp, and nearby was a row of white wooden boxes. All around they could hear a faint buzzing noise. Elizabeth's heart began to beat faster.

"What's that sound?" Jessica whispered.

"I'm not sure," Elizabeth said.

"What is all this stuff?" Lila asked, looking nervously at the equipment.

Everyone turned to look at Andy. He was the best science student in their class. Elizabeth hoped he would be able to figure out what all these strange things were.

Andy was smiling. He walked right up to a box topped by a spinning antenna and examined it closely. "I know what this is," he said, sounding excited.

He stood up, looked around at the others and took a deep breath. "It's a probe."

Elizabeth's heart skipped a beat. Lila's mouth dropped open.

"What do you mean, a probe?" Charlie asked. He backed up a step.

Andy switched on his tape recorder. "An

alien probe sent to collect data about Earth."
He began taking pictures of the equipment.

"Come on," Todd said with a nervous laugh. "You're kidding, right?"

"Don't tease us, Andy," Jessica said.

Elizabeth didn't know what to think. The buzzing sound that was all around them made it difficult to concentrate. All she knew for sure was that she was getting frightened.

"This is probably picking up TV and radio signals and sending them back to the main UFO station," Andy explained, pointing to the antenna. He bent forward to look at a needle under a glass window that was drawing a jagged line as the paper rolled under it. Every few seconds, the needle zigzagged sharply and then went straight again. "I'm not sure what this is doing," he said. "But it sure looks interesting. These aliens must be very scientifically advanced."

"Do you think he means it?" Todd whispered in Elizabeth's ear.

Elizabeth wiped her hands on her jeans. She was so nervous that her palms were sweating. "I don't know," she whispered back. "He does know a lot about these things."

"I don't like this," Todd said, looking over his shoulder to make sure that no aliens were creeping up behind him.

Jessica folded her arms across her chest and squeezed her eyes shut. "Well, I don't believe it," she said in a frightened voice. "I just don't believe it. There's no such things as aliens. No way."

The buzzing sound seemed to come and go. The sun beat down, making Elizabeth feel hot and tired and afraid.

Could Andy be right?

CHAPTER 6

Broken Parts

Jessica felt a shiver go up her back. The strange buzzing sound was giving her the creeps. It seemed to be loudest near the row of white wooden boxes. Minute by minute, Jessica became more certain that they really were standing in front of an alien space probe.

"Let's get out of here," she begged. "We can tell the teachers about this. They'll know what to do."

"I have to take some pictures first," Andy

said. He circled around the probe, his camera clicking.

"What if one of the—you know," Charlie said hoarsely. "What if one of them comes?"

Jessica's stomach did a roller-coaster dive. "You mean one of the aliens?"

She took a quick look around the clearing. If an alien appeared, she knew she would jump ten feet in the air. For now though, she backed up a little bit, then gasped as the back of her leg bumped into one of the pieces of equipment.

"I touched it," she said, her eyes wide.

"Is your skin dissolving?" Charlie asked, taking a quick step away from her.

Jessica bent to examine her leg. "Not yet," she whispered.

At that moment, one of the pieces of the

probe began to tick slowly. Everyone froze and stared at it. The clicking sped up, until it sounded like a stopwatch. Then it stopped. All was silent.

Suddenly, a high-pitched whine pierced the air. Jessica jumped back in surprise. She bumped into Charlie, who stumbled and knocked over one of the pieces of equipment. It fell on its side on the ground. Instantly, the whining stopped.

Jessica's heart was pounding. "You broke it," she said, sounding terrified. She looked as if she were about to burst into tears.

"Me?" Charlie said. "You bumped into me! It's your fault."

"It was an accident," Elizabeth said quickly.

Andy was staring at the broken part of the

alien probe. "Wow," he said. "They're really going to be mad about this."

"Maybe they won't notice," Lila said. "We haven't seen anyone—"

"So far," Charlie interrupted. "Do you think they'll come and find us?" he asked Andy. Andy shrugged and turned away to take another picture.

"Charlie did it, not me," Jessica said again, her voice quivering.

Charlie stood up and faced her angrily. "If they get me, they'll get you, too!"

"Maybe we can fix it," Todd suggested. "Help me stand it up again."

"Come on, let's just get out of here," Lila said. "I bet Mrs. Otis is looking for us."

"You're just scared, Lila," Jessica said.

"So are you!" Lila yelled.

"I don't think—" Elizabeth began, but she stopped talking in mid-sentence.

Jessica and the others turned to see what was wrong. Elizabeth was staring over at the woods on the far side of the meadow. Her face was pale. With a pounding heart, Jessica looked there, too.

A tall figure was walking toward them. It was dressed in what looked like a space suit, with a strange hood on its head. Jessica's mouth opened and closed, but not a single sound came out.

Then Lila began to scream.

CHAPTER 7

Run!

As Lila screamed, Elizabeth stared in horror. She felt as if her legs had suddenly turned to stone, and she couldn't move. It was worse than the worst nightmare she'd ever had.

The figure strode toward them. In one hand it carried something that looked like a gun. Puffs of smoke came out of the weapon.

"An alien!" Lila screeched. "It's really an alien!"

"It's coming right at us!" Charlie shouted.

"Let's get out of here!" Jessica yelled. She grabbed Elizabeth's hand and yanked her backward. Elizabeth stumbled, but she caught herself before she fell. She couldn't stop staring at the approaching alien.

"Liz! Come on!" Jessica said in a terrified voice.

Charlie, Lila, and Todd were already running back the way they had come. Jessica pulled at Elizabeth's hand again, and finally Elizabeth's legs started working. The twins began sprinting after the others. Elizabeth's heart was beating so hard she could feel it pounding inside her chest.

"It's going to zap us," Jessica sobbed. "Run faster!"

Elizabeth raced beside her sister toward the woods. She had never been so frightened in her whole life. The edge of the forest was just a short distance away and the others were already dashing into the trees.

"Come on, hurry!" Todd yelled.

With one hand out to push the branches aside, Elizabeth ran into the dimness of the forest. Jessica was close behind. They soon caught up to their friends, who had stopped a short distance into the trees.

"Was this the way we came before?" Lila asked, looking from side to side.

"I can't remember," Charlie said. He was breathing hard. "How do we get back to the lake?"

Todd turned around. "Andy, do you—" He broke off and spun around again. "Andy?"

Elizabeth felt cold, then hot, then cold again. Andy wasn't with them.

"Where is he?" Jessica whispered.

"Andy?" Lila called.

Elizabeth looked back through the trees. "Didn't he come with us?" she asked.

They all stared at one another. Nobody said a word for a minute.

Then Jessica began to cry. "Oh, no!" she wailed. "We're never going to see him again."

"Don't say that," Elizabeth said. She turned to Todd. "Come on." She started toward the clearing.

"Liz, don't go!" Jessica said. She grabbed Elizabeth's hand to stop her.

"Andy might be in trouble," Elizabeth said, pulling her hand away.

Todd nodded and gulped. "He might need help."

Elizabeth crept silently toward the edge of

the woods. The others crowded close behind her as she reached forward to push aside the branches that were blocking their view of the clearing. When she did so, they all saw a terrifying sight. Andy was standing in the middle of the clearing next to the alien probe, watching the alien approach.

"It's going to get him," Lila whispered.

Step by step, the alien came closer. The smoke continued to puff out of the weapon in its hand. Andy didn't move.

Elizabeth closed her eyes. She couldn't bear to watch anymore.

CHAPTER 8

Captured!

Jessica bit her lip to stop herself from screaming. She was sure that Andy was about to be vaporized before their very eyes.

"Why doesn't he run away?" Charlie whispered.

"He isn't afraid," Todd said, in an admiring voice.

The alien took one last step and stood in front of Andy.

Trying not to cry, Jessica covered her eyes

with her hands. But she had to see what was happening. She peeked out from between her fingers.

"He's talking to it," Elizabeth said.

They saw Andy point to the broken piece of equipment. He seemed to be explaining what had happened. Then he turned and pointed toward the woods where they were hiding, and Jessica covered her eyes again in terror.

"What do you think they're talking about?" Todd asked quietly.

"Maybe Andy's trying to make friends," Elizabeth said.

Charlie was shaking his head. "I can't believe it. Andy isn't one bit scared."

"Do you think the alien understands him?"

Lila asked. "I didn't know they spoke English in outer space."

"Go on and find out if you're so curious," Charlied snapped at her.

"No way." Lila backed up. "You go."

"He must be asking what all the equipment is for," Jessica whispered.

"Maybe," Elizabeth said. "Look, the alien is pointing at those white boxes."

Jessica stared. Part of her wanted to run away, but she was curious, too. She wondered what Andy and the alien were talking about.

Suddenly, the alien raised its smoking weapon. "Oh, no!" Jessica said. "Look out!"

"He's not aiming it at Andy," Todd said.

"Maybe there are more aliens in those boxes," Charlie suggested. "Maybe they get big when the lids open. That guy could be their leader, and he might be about to let them out."

"That's dumb," Lila said. But she sounded very uncertain.

Jessica was staring at Andy. She was amazed at how calm he was. He didn't act frightened at all. In fact, she could see him smiling at the alien.

"Andy is awfully brave. I'll never make fun of him again," Jessica said.

"*If* he makes it back alive," Charlie said.

Elizabeth turned to frown at him. "That's a horrible thing to say. I think we should try to help him."

"But, Liz," Jessica began. "What if—"

"Look!" Lila gasped.

They turned to look again. The alien was pointing in the direction from which it had come.

"He must be pointing toward where his spaceship is parked," Todd whispered.

"Andy isn't going with him, is he?" Elizabeth asked fearfully.

Jessica's heartbeat thudded in her ears. The suspense was terrible. As they all watched, the alien put its arm across Andy's shoulders.

"He's being kidnapped!" Lila moaned.

"What are we going to do?" Jessica asked, tears springing back to her eyes again. "The alien will probably take him back to his planet and put him in a zoo. We'll never see him again!"

"I'm going to save him," Elizabeth announced suddenly.

Jessica got goose bumps up and down her arms. "No, Liz! Don't go! It'll get you, too!"

But there was nothing she could do. Before Jessica could stop her, Elizabeth stepped out of the trees into the clearing.

CHAPTER 9

Under the Hood

Elizabeth had only one thing on her mind. She couldn't let the alien capture Andy.

"Stop! Stop!" she yelled, running toward them as fast as she could. "Leave Andy here!"

Andy and the alien turned at the sound of her shouts. The alien put down the smoking space weapon and raised its arms to its neck.

"It's taking off its head!" Charlie yelled from back in the woods. At that, Jessica and

Lila and Todd couldn't stay quiet any longer. They all started screaming at the tops of their lungs.

Elizabeth stopped in her tracks and stared in horror as the alien slowly removed the hood of its space suit. Elizabeth had a good imagination, but what was happening before her eyes was much stranger and more frightening than anything she could possibly imagine.

But the strangest thing of all was that Andy was still smiling.

When the alien raised its hood over its head, Elizabeth was shocked. It looked exactly like a human being.

"What—wait a second," Elizabeth stammered. She was completely confused.

The others ran up to join her. Andy was

looking at them with a cheerful, mischievous smile on his face.

"Hi," said the alien in a man's voice.

"Hi," Elizabeth repeated, still puzzled. She looked at Andy, who smiled even wider.

"I'm Mr. Lowman," the alien said with a friendly nod at them. "What seems to be the trouble?"

"Aren't you from outer space? "Jessica asked.

Mr. Lowman and Andy looked at each other and grinned. Then Andy burst out laughing.

"You guys really thought this was an alien probe!" he said. "I thought you didn't believe in UFOs!"

"But . . ." Elizabeth looked at Mr. Lowman. Then she began to smile, too.

"I'm the park ranger," Mr. Lowman explained with a chuckle. "This is my weather station. Those white boxes contain several hives of bees."

Suddenly Elizabeth understood. "Bees! That's what that buzzing sound is."

"Mr. Lowman has to wear that suit when he gets the honey, so the bees don't sting him," Andy explained. "And the smoke gun is to make them fly away while he's doing it."

Lila's face was pink with embarrassment. "I knew that," she said in a loud voice.

"No, you didn't," Andy said. "You were scared to death. But I knew all along what this stuff was."

Elizabeth couldn't help laughing. Andy had gotten even with them all for teasing him about UFOs. She felt silly for being so frightened of a weather station and some beehives.

"So you weren't really brave after all," Charlie said. "You didn't stand up to a space creature."

"But he stayed to tell Mr. Lowman that we knocked over his equipment," Todd pointed out. "That was brave."

"Hey, that's right," Jessica said. "I wouldn't have done that."

Andy smiled and shrugged.

"Did we break anything?" Elizabeth asked Mr. Lowman. "We didn't mean to."

The park ranger shook his head. Now that they knew he wasn't an alien, he seemed very nice. "There doesn't seem to be any

damage. Would you like to know what these instruments do? I've already shown Andy, so maybe he'd like to tell you himself."

Looking very proud and happy, Andy began to explain how the weather station equipment worked. There were instruments to measure the wind, the temperature, and the rainfall. The box with the moving needle recorded the information automatically.

"Now I think it's time for you kids to be getting back to the lake," Mr. Lowman said when Andy had finished talking. "Your teachers are probably worried."

Elizabeth and Jessica looked at each other nervously. Aliens or no aliens, they still didn't know the way back to the lake!

CHAPTER 10

The Big Race

Jessica looked back at the woods. "We're lost," she told Mr. Lowman. "We don't know how to get back."

"Didn't you follow trail markers?" the ranger asked.

They all shook their heads. "We didn't go on a trail," Todd admitted.

"There's a trail entrance right over here," Mr. Lowman said. "I'll take you back."

"Thanks, Mr. Lowman," Andy said. "I'm

glad you found us. It's been a very interesting afternoon."

Jessica snuck a look at Andy. She was surprised at how much he really knew about things. She was also surprised that he had stayed behind to tell Mr. Lowman about knocking over the weather station equipment. Maybe he wasn't a complete goofball after all, even if he did believe in UFOs.

Mr. Lowman led them to a winding trail not far from their hiding place. Every ten feet, there was a square piece of bright red plastic nailed to a tree to mark the trail. Mr. Lowman told them that all the hiking and nature trails in the woods were marked that way so that people wouldn't get lost. In a few minutes, Secca Lake came into view.

"I hope we don't get in trouble," Lila said

as they heard the happy shouts of students in the distance.

Jessica crossed her fingers behind her back for good luck. "Me, too."

"Look," Caroline Pearce shouted. "There they are!"

Mrs. Otis and several other teachers and students were standing in a group near the end of the trail. Mrs. Otis let out a sigh of relief. "Thank goodness you're safe. We were about to send out a search party."

To Jessica's amazement, Andy stepped forward. "It's my fault," he said. "I was looking for signs of UFOs, and they came with me."

"They're just fine," Mr. Lowman said, stepping forward to shake Mrs. Otis's hand. "My name is Bert Lowman. I'm the ranger here."

"I'm glad you found each other," Mrs. Otis

said, shaking her head. She looked upset, but relieved. "I was very worried about you kids."

"We're sorry, Mrs. Otis," Elizabeth said.

"Yes, we're sorry," Jessica repeated in a timid voice. "We won't do it again."

"I'm glad to hear that," Mrs. Otis said. "Next time I might not be so understanding."

"Like Andy said, it was his fault," Charlie said. "Him and his stupid UFOs."

Mr. Lowman shook his head. "Now, don't say that, young man. There have been some very strange sightings up here in the past. Quite a few scientific teams have done research in this area. They haven't found any evidence of extraterrestrial visitors yet, but you should keep an open mind."

Everyone turned to look at Andy. He

smiled at Mr. Lowman, and Jessica felt a shiver go up her back. Maybe Andy would become a scientist one day. And maybe *he* would discover evidence of life in outer space.

After they had a drink and a few minutes to rest, it was time for the last race of the day.

"It's the three-legged race," Elizabeth said to Jessica. "I hope all our practicing pays off."

"Me, too," Jessica replied.

"OK. Line up two by two," Mr. Cutler called out. "Mrs. Otis and I will come around to tie your legs together."

Jessica stood on Elizabeth's right side. Then she walked around and stood on Elizabeth's left side. "Which is better?" she asked.

"We practiced this way," Elizabeth said,

moving so that Jessica was on her right side again.

As Mr. Cutler tied their middle legs together with two pieces of red yarn, Jessica concentrated on the finish line. In a moment, everything was ready. Mr. Cutler raised his hand. "On your marks . . . Get set . . . GO!"

"Come on!" Jessica yelled.

"One-two, one-two," Elizabeth counted.

Being twins gave them a special edge. All of the other pairs had trouble getting their steps timed just right, but Jessica and Elizabeth ran together perfectly.

"Go, go, go!" Mrs. Otis shouted. "Come on, twins!"

"One-two, one—we did it!" Jessica screamed as they stepped over the finish line ahead of all the others. They flopped over together onto the grass.

"You know what we should do?" Elizabeth said breathlessly. She began to untie their straps. "When we go on our vacation to the Grand Canyon, we can go three-legged."

Jessica laughed. "Maybe we can even get twin pack mules for the ride into the canyon and get them to go three-legged."

"Wait a minute." Elizabeth frowned and counted on her fingers. "They'd have to go six-legged. Or would it be seven-legged?"

Jessica laughed even harder. She loved being silly with her sister, and she was sure they'd have plenty of opportunities to be silly together on their family vacation. They were going to Arizona to see the Grand Canyon.

"We'll have the best time," Jessica said. "And we'll do everything together."

How well will Jessica and Elizabeth get along on the family trip? Find out in Sweet Valley Kids #30, JESSICA'S UNBURIED TREASURE.